Best Loved

FAIRY TALES

Published by Chartwell Books Inc.
A Division of Book Sales Inc.
110 Enterprise Avenue
Secaucus, New Jersey 07094

ISBN 0-89009-243-5
Library of Congress 79-514-73

Colour reproduction by Metric Reproductions Ltd.
Filmset by Photographics
Printed in Italy by New Interlitho Sp A.
Published in England 1979 by Sackett and
Marshall Ltd., 2 Great Marlborough Street,
London W.1, England.

Best Loved FAIRY TALES

Retold by Lis Robson

Illustrated by Teddy Williams

CHARTWELL BOOKS INC.

Contents

Cinderella

Once upon a time, in a distant country a little girl lived with her Father and Mother in a beautiful house. They were a happy family, but when little Ella was still small, her mother died. Some years later her father married again—a handsome widow with two daughters, Serephina and Hermione. They were rather plain, but very proud and vain, and as Ella grew and became more beautiful they came to hate her. Her stepmother made her do all the housework, and she was called Cinderella because she was always covered with ashes and cinders from the fire.

One day an invitation came from the palace. The king was giving a ball in honor of his son, the prince, who had come of age and was to choose a wife. The stepsisters were delirious with excitement and planned what they were going to wear.

"I shall wear pink satin with green lace," said Serephina—a most unsuitable choice, as she had bright red hair and was long and skinny.

"And I shall wear baby-blue lace and sweet little roses," said Hermione, who was equally tall, but extremely fat.

"But what shall I wear?" asked Cinderella timidly. Both sisters stared at her.

"You're not coming to the ball. How could we dream of taking such a dirty little servant with us?"

Poor Cinderella, for the next few days she was rushing around pinning up dresses, sewing on lace, finding gloves and shoes and doing her stepsisters' hair. At last the night of the ball came. The stepmother and stepsisters were all dressed in their finery and the coach carried them off to the palace. Cinderella was left, sad and forlorn, sitting by the great fireplace in the kitchen. Tears began to flow and Cinderella cried as she thought of the wonderful time the guests would have and of the handsome young prince.

Then came a crash and a flash, and an old woman in a cloak and pointed hat stood in front of her.

"Who are you?" gasped Cinderella.

"I am your fairy godmother," said she. "Why are you crying child?"

"I want to go to the ball," said Cinderella.

"So you shall my dear," said the fairy godmother. "Run and fetch me a pumpkin." So Cinderella went and picked the largest pumpkin she could find. The fairy godmother pointed her wand at it and woosh! there stood a beautiful golden coach.

"Now fetch me six mice, three rats and a lizard," said the fairy godmother.

Cinderella quickly found the animals and returned to the kitchen. The fairy godmother turned the mice into beautiful white horses, the rats into footmen, and the

lizard into a coachman.

"Now, Cinderella," she cried, "you must have a dress." She waved her wand and Cinderella was clad in a magnificent ball-gown of white silk, and on her feet were the sweetest glass slippers.

"Go to the ball Cinderella and dance with the prince, but you must be home by midnight as the spell ends then."

Cinderella thanked the fairy godmother, and drove off in the coach to the palace.

When she arrived at the palace and entered the ballroom, all the guests stopped dancing and looked at the beautiful girl in the shimmering ballgown.

The prince fell in love with her straight away and danced every dance with her.

"What is your name, where do you come from?" he asked her, but Cinderella would not tell him. She was so happy dancing with the prince that she forgot the fairy godmother's warning, and all too soon the chimes of the palace clock told her it was midnight. Cinderella fled from the palace, down the long staircase, losing one of her glass slippers as she ran.

As she reached the bottom of the staircase, her ballgown changed to rags, the coach into the pumpkin, and the horses, coachman and footmen became, once more the mice, the lizards and the rats.

The next day the prince was in despair. Where was his beautiful princess—all that was left was a tiny glass slipper. So the royal herald proclaimed throughout the town that "Whosoever the slipper fitted would be the prince's bride."

The slipper was carried to every house in the town, and tried by every lady, but it fitted none of them. At last the royal party reached the house where Cinderella lived. The stepmother and stepsisters were greatly excited – surely the slipper would fit one of them. The stepmother tried it first, but her feet were so lumpy and bumpy that only one toe would go in. Then Serephina tried it, but her feet were so long and thin, that it dangled off the end. Lastly, Hermione tried the slipper on, but her feet were so fat that, try as she might, she could not cram them in.

Then Cinderella came forward and asked if she might try it on. The stepmother and sisters scoffed at her, but the royal herald—who was very tired of ladies feet by now—said "Every lady must try it."

So Cinderella put out her dainty foot; the slipper fitted perfectly. She then produced the matching slipper from her pocket. The prince claimed her as his bride. They were married in great splendor and lived happily ever after.

Red Riding Hood

Once upon a time a little girl lived with her mother and father in a pretty little cottage on the edge of a forest. Her mother made her a cloak and hood of warm red wool and from then on she was known as Red Riding Hood.

One day her mother packed up a basket full of new laid eggs, a loaf of bread and some cakes and asked Red Riding Hood to take them to her grandmother, who was ill. She lived in a cottage on the other side of the forest.

"Go straight to your grandmother's," said Red Riding Hood's mother, "and don't speak to anyone on the way there."

Red Riding Hood walked happily through the forest —it was a warm bright day, the birds were singing and little woodland animals came out from the shelter of the trees to see her. Halfway through the forest Red Riding Hood stopped to pick her grandmother some flowers. She wandered off the path into the trees and came face to face with a large wolf.

"Good morning my dear," said the wolf, very politely. "Where are you off to on such a fine day?"

"I'm taking this basket of goodies to my grandmother, who is ill," said Red Riding Hood. "Her cottage is on the

other side of the forest," added the foolish girl.

"Well my dear," said the crafty old wolf, "let's have a race to your grandmother's cottage. You go along the path and I will go through the trees and we will see who arrives there first."

So Red Riding Hood skipped off along the path and the wolf slipped into the trees and ran as quickly as he could to grandmother's cottage.

When he arrived he banged on the door.

"Who is it?" asked the feeble voice of Red Riding Hood's grandmother.

"It's Red Riding Hood," said the wolf in a high sweet voice. "I've come to see you, grandmother, and bring you a basket of goodies."

"Come in my dear," said grandmother, and the wolf opened the door, rushed up to grandmother's bed and in no time at all had gobbled her up. He then put on grandmother's nightgown, nightcap, and glasses and got into bed to wait for Red Riding Hood. Not long after Red Riding Hood knocked on the door.

"Who is there?" asked the wolf in a feeble old voice just like grandmother's.

"It's little Red Riding Hood," said the child. "Can I come in? I have a basket of goodies to help make you feel better."

"Come in my dear," said the wolf.

Red Riding Hood lifted up the latch and entered.

She went up to the bed and, oh my, grandmother did look strange.

"What big eyes you have today, grandmother," said

Red Riding Hood beginning to feel worried.

"All the better to see you with my dear," said the wolf.

"What big ears you have today, grandmother," said Red Riding Hood.

"All the better to hear you with my dear," said the wolf.

"What big teeth you have today, grandmother," said Red Riding Hood.

"All the better to eat you with," said the wolf and sprang out of bed and tried to catch Red Riding Hood.

But with loud screams Red Riding Hood ran out of the door and into the forest. The noise was heard by a woodman who came to her rescue. He chopped the wolf in half and out jumped grandmother, very upset but quite unharmed as the wolf had hastily swallowed her whole.

They all sat down and ate the cakes Red Riding Hood's mother had sent. Then the woodman took Red Riding Hood home to her mother. Whenever she went to grandmother's cottage she stayed on the path and never ever talked to strangers.

Aladdin

Once upon a time, in a country called China, there lived a boy named Aladdin. His mother was a washerwoman. As they were very poor, she worked very hard all day long. Aladdin was not fond of working, though, and would spend most of the day dreaming of the riches he would some day possess and of the beautiful princess he wanted to marry.

One day, as Aladdin was sitting on the doorstep, idly dreaming, a tall, dark, sinister-looking man came up to him.

"You must be Aladdin, my dead brother's son," said the man. "I am your long lost uncle."

Aladdin took him in to his mother. The uncle sat and talked of the many lands he had wandered through and the fabulous sights he had seen.

Then he said to Aladdin, very temptingly, "If you come with me, I will help you find jewels and riches beyond your dreams."

Aladdin very quickly agreed to go with his uncle and they set off through the city, beyond the gates and into the barren, lonely country. At last they reached a strange, rocky valley. Here the uncle halted by the side

of a cliff. He lit a fire on the ground and spoke some odd sounding words over it. A small opening appeared in the cliff face. Aladdin began to feel rather frightened.

"If you go into the cave," said the uncle, "you will find great quantities of treasure. Take what you like, but be sure to find a small lamp that is in there and bring it to me. Take this ring, it will keep you from harm."

Poor Aladdin; down he went into the darkness until he came to a large cavern filled with sparkling jewels and precious metals. He stood and marvelled at the fortune displayed before him, then remembered the lamp his uncle wanted. He searched through the cavern until he found the small dusty lamp. He made his way back to the entrance and called to his uncle, "I have found the lamp, please let me out."

"Give me the lamp first," cried his uncle.

"No, no," said Aladdin, "help me to get out."

But the uncle, who was really an evil magician, wanted only the lamp. When Aladdin refused to hand it to him he closed the opening and left Aladdin alone in the dark cave.

Aladdin was terrified. Alone in such a place, he was sure to die. Then he remembered the ring and gently rubbed it. To his amazement a large genie appeared.

The genie told Aladdin he was the slave of the ring and would grant him any wish.

"Take me home," cried Aladdin. No sooner had he said this, than he found himself at home. He told his mother of his adventure and showed her the lamp.

"Well," said his mother, "we can at least sell this in

the market." And she began to polish it. But as soon as she rubbed it, a gigantic genie appeared, and announced himself the slave of the lamp.

"I can grant your heart's desire," said he.

Aladdin and his mother ordered food, which arrived on gold and silver plates. After living this way for some weeks, Aladdin's thoughts began to dwell on the Emperor's beautiful daughter. He would marry her at once. He ordered the genie to bring as much treasure as he could. Then he sent it all to the palace, saying it was a gift from Aladdin to the Emperor and asking for the hand of the princess. The Emperor was delighted at the thought of such a wealthy son-in-law and happily gave his consent.

Aladdin and the princess were married and lived very happily in a magnificent palace provided by the genie of the lamp. They made good use of their wealth and were very generous to the poor of the city.

The wicked magician, however, had not given up hope of possessing the lamp. And one day, when Aladdin was away from the palace, he came to the door disguised as a lamp seller. The princess ran to the window, saw the bright new lamps and called to a maid.

"Take that dirty old lamp my husband has in his room and exchange it for a new one."

As soon as the magician had it in his grasp he ordered the genie to transport the palace and its occupants to Africa.

Aladdin was in despair when he returned, but summoned the genie of the ring.

"Restore the princess to me," he begged, but the genie said only the genie of the lamp could do that. All he could do was take him to Africa.

So Aladdin found himself in Africa near to his palace. He ran into the palace and found his princess weeping bitterly. She begged Aladdin's forgiveness for her foolishness and said that he must get the lamp back and break the magician's power.

Aladdin gave the princess some sleeping powders and told her to put them in the magician's wine that evening. When the magician came home he ordered the princess to bring him fruit and wine. After drinking the wine he fell onto the floor in a deep sleep. Aladdin rushed in and chopped off the magician's head. Then he took the lamp, rubbed it and told the genie to take them back to China. The princess and Aladdin lived in great happiness. The lamp was placed on a velvet cushion and guarded very carefully by two soldiers.

The Sleeping Beauty

In a distant kingdom there once lived a King and Queen in a beautiful castle with splendid turrets and towers and a beautiful garden all around it. But they were not completely happy as they had no children. Then one summer's day the Queen gave birth to a little baby girl. The King and Queen rejoiced and all their courtiers and subjects with them.

"We will have a magnificent christening," cried the King, "and as well as all our courtiers and subjects, we will ask all the good fairies we know."

So the invitations were sent out and a great feast prepared. The christening day dawned warm and bright and all the guests started arriving at the palace. The baby was christened with the names Briar Rose and, after the fine banquet had been eaten, presents were given to the princess.

The courtiers and loyal subjects gave the usual silver mugs, spoons and rattles; but the fairies' presents were quite different. One said that the princess would be as beautiful as the dawn. Another said she would be good and kind, another that she would sing like a nightingale, yet another that she would dance as lightly as

thistledown. Just as the last fairy came forward to bestow her gift upon the baby, a great flash of light came into the banqueting hall, followed by a terrible roaring noise and a black, awful figure appeared. It was Carabosse, the oldest and nastiest of all the fairies. The Royal Chamberlain had forgotten to send her an invitation to the christening. She was in a terrible rage. Advancing across the floor towards the baby's cradle, she hissed, "I shall give your little darling a gift, although I have been ignored. She shall live until she is sixteen in beauty and grace, but then she will prick her finger on a spindle and die." And with a hideous laugh Carabosse disappeared.

The King and his Queen were stricken with grief and terror, but the last fairy stepped forward and said, "I cannot take away the spell that Carabosse has laid, but my gift to the little princess will be that, when she pricks her finger, she will not die but fall into a sleep for a hundred years and be awoken by the kiss of a prince."

But the King could not forget the wicked fairy's words and ordered all the spinning wheels in the country to be burnt.

Little Briar Rose grew to be as beautiful and good as the fairies had promised. As the years went by everyone forgot the awful curse laid upon her by Carabosse and because of the King's order Briar Rose had never seen a spinning wheel.

On her sixteenth birthday she was wandering round the garden as she had been told to keep out of the palace because of all the surprises being prepared for her. She was becoming rather bored when she came across a

small door at the bottom of a tower. She opened the door and, finding a winding flight of stairs, climbed them. At the top was another little door which Briar Rose opened. Inside the small dusty room was a tiny old woman sitting at a spinning wheel. As Briar Rose had never seen one before she politely asked the old woman what it was and how it was used.

"Sit down my dear," said the old woman, "and I will show you. Take the spindle in your hand." As Briar Rose took hold of the spindle she felt a sharp prick and instantly fell into a deep sleep. The old woman straightaway turned into the Fairy Carabosse and, gleefully thinking that Briar Rose was dead, flew off out of the window.

The princess was soon missed and a great search was organized. Eventually they found her lying as if dead in the tower. They carried her down to the King and Queen who were overcome with misery and wept bitterly. While they were weeping the good fairy entered and cast a spell over the palace and all it's inhabitants. Now they would all sleep with the princess for a hundred years. From the King and Queen down to the smallest fly in the stables every living thing shut it's eyes and fell into a deep slumber. Around the castle and gardens an immense hedge of briar roses grew until nothing could could be seen but the highest tower.

During the hundred years of the spell the tales and legends of the sleeping beauty, who lay in a castle behind a briar hedge, spread to many kingdoms. Young princes dreamt of rescuing this princess and set out bravely and merrily on their venture. But none of them could ever

penetrate the thick hedge around the castle and emerged very sore from the many scratches from the monstrous thorns.

Then one morning a young prince arrived at the briar hedge. He was very handsome and very determined He unsheathed his sword and prepared to slash his way through; but to his amazement the thick branches and thorns melted before him. He found himself in the gardens of the palace—there was no sound anywhere, even the birds were asleep in the trees. He walked up the steps into the palace and saw before him the princess asleep on a silken bed, with her parents and all the courtiers around her. The prince crept up to her, bent gently down and kissed her. The princess slowly opened her eyes and fell instantly in love with the prince. The spell was broken and everyone woke up. The King and Queen rejoiced to find their daughter alive and well and soon consented to the marriage of Briar Rose to her handsome prince. The wedding took place in three days, and they all lived happily ever after.

The Frog Prince

There once lived, in the most beautiful castle you can imagine, a pretty little princess. She had long brown curls and velvet brown eyes, and loved to dance and play all day; but she was rather spoilt. Everyone in the castle was expected to do exactly as the little princess wanted and she very seldom thought about other peoples' feelings and wishes.

One day the princess was playing in the castle garden. It was a lovely garden, full of scented flowers, shady trees, lily ponds and sparkling fountains. The princess was tossing into the air a ball made of spun gold and catching it. The ball had been a birthday gift and the princess thought it was the most beautiful ball she had ever seen. But while she was playing the princess slipped on the grass and the ball flew into the middle of a lily pond and disappeared. The princess was horrified and burst into loud sobs as she sat down at the edge of the pond.

At last a voice was heard above her sobbing.

"Whatever is the matter?" croaked the voice, "I have never heard such a wailing in all my life. Are you in pain or has someone hurt you?"

The princess looked up and to her amazement she saw a large green bull-frog sitting by her.

"I've lost my golden ball," said the princess. "It has fallen into the pond and sunk to the bottom and I can't get it out."

"Oh, is that all," croaked the frog, and prepared to jump back into the pond.

"Aren't you going to help me?" cried the princess. "I'll do anything you ask if you will fetch my ball for me."

"Will you indeed?" said the frog. "Then I might consider helping you." He thought for a little while and then he said, "If I rescue your ball will you grant me three favor?"

"Anything you ask," said the princess, "just get my ball for me."

"Very well," said the frog. "I want to come to the castle, sit by you at dinner, eat from your plate and sleep on your silken pillow at night."

The princess was extremely upset at the frog's requests—she did not enjoy the thought of sharing either her dinner or her bed with a large green frog; but as there seemed no other way to retrieve her ball she reluctantly agreed.

The frog jumped into the pond and found the ball. He brought it back to the princess, who thanked him and ran quickly back to the castle. She promptly forgot all about the frog and the promises she had made and was horrified when at dinner the frog appeared at her side.

"Go away," she said, "you can't sit here."

"Indeed I can," said the frog. "We made a bargain.

I've kept my side of it, now you must keep yours," and he moved nearer to the princess.

When dinner was served the frog hopped on to the table and helped himself to the delicious food from the princess's plate. The princess was furious, but the frog reminded her of their bargain.

When the meal was over the princess hurried away to her bedroom hoping that this terrible wet green creature would not follow. But when she got into bed the frog was there on her pillow. The poor princess burst into tears and implored the frog to go away.

"Very well," said the frog sadly, "I will not stay with someone who finds me so repulsive, although I did them such a kindness."

The princess, seeing the frog so unhappy, felt very ashamed and begged the frog to forgive her. She bent down and softly kissed the top of his wet green head. To the princess's astonishment the frog instantly changed into a handsome prince. He knelt before her and thanked her for saving him, saying that he had been under the spell of an evil witch and could only become a prince again if he was kissed by a kindhearted princess.

The prince and princess fell in love and soon after were married. The princess learnt to consider other people's feelings and became a much nicer and happier princess.

Hansel and Gretel

There once lived a poor woodcutter who had two children, Hansel and Gretel. Their mother had died and their stepmother was an unpleasant woman.

The family were very poor and soon there was little money or food left in the house. One night the stepmother said to the woodcutter, "We cannot live like this any longer. If we did not have the children we would fare better. Tomorrow we must take them far into the forest and leave them there."

The woodcutter was horrified, but the more he argued against the plan the more angry the stepmother became. Hansel and Gretel, lying in bed, heard their father and stepmother shouting and trembled with fear. Gretel cried bitterly but Hansel said, "Don't cry, I have thought of a plan that will help us find our way home."

When the cottage was quiet, Hansel got out of bed and went silently out of the back door. In the garden he found some pebbles which he put into his pocket.

Early the next morning the stepmother called the children to hurry and dress as they were going in the forest to help their father collect sticks. Hansel dropped the pebbles behind him as they walked through the forest

so that their way home would be marked. In the very heart of the forest the woodcutter and his wife sat down to rest and told the children to start gathering sticks. The children were so busy that they did not see their parents steal quietly away. As it became dark they realized they were alone and Gretel became very frightened. But Hansel showed her the trail of pebbles and following these they returned safely home.

The stepmother was not pleased to see them. Soon afterwards, when there was nothing in the house but one stale loaf of bread, she again persuaded the woodcutter to leave the children in the forest. As before the children heard all that was said and Hansel crept downstairs, only to find all the doors locked. So the next morning when the stepmother gave him his slice of bread, he crumbled it and put the crumbs in his pocket. As they walked along he dropped the crumbs behind him. But alas for Hansel and Gretel, when they tried to find their way home they discovered that birds had eaten all the crumbs.

The children were frightened and lonely in the deep, dark forest, but Hansel found a soft bed of leaves and moss for Gretel and himself. Clasped in each other's arms they slept through the night. In the morning they wandered through the forest, very sad and hungry. Suddenly they came across a tiny cottage made of gingerbread. The children ran to it and started eating pieces of this strange house. The door of the house flew open and out came an old woman. Hansel and Gretel dropped their cake but the old woman smiled and invited them in.

"Come in and stay with me dear children," she said. "You can eat all your heart desires."

The children followed her in and were soon tucking in to a most fantastic feast. The old woman showed them into the sweetest little bedroom and in the soft white beds they soon fell asleep.

But the old woman was really a wicked witch and during the night she pulled Hansel from his bed and locked him in a cage. In the morning she told Gretel that she must help her to cook lots of food for Hansel to make him fat and juicy. "I shall eat him and then it will be your turn." Poor Gretel pleaded with the witch for mercy, but the cruel witch only laughed and told Gretel to fetch water from the well.

She kept Hansel in the cage for a week and then one morning she told Gretel that she was going to eat Hansel that day, whether he was fat enough or not.

"Creep inside the oven, child," she told Gretel, "and see if it is hot enough."

But Gretel realizing that the witch meant to roast her, pretended to be stupid and said she did not know how. So the witch grumbling all the while, climbed in to show Gretel, who pushed her in and shut the oven doors. Then she set Hansel free. They searched the house and found many chests of jewels. They filled their pockets and then set off on their way home. On reaching their cottage they found their father alone, for the stepmother had died. Their father was overjoyed to see them and with all the witch's jewels they lived in comfort and were very happy.

Rumpelstiltskin

In a distant country there once lived a vain and boastful miller. He had one daughter who was very beautiful.

One day the miller was walking through the wood when he came face to face with the King of that country. The miller bowed low to the King and moved aside to let him pass, but the King thought he should have a talk with one of his subjects.

"Who are you?" said the King.

"I am a miller," said the miller.

"Have you any family?" inquired the King, and the miller wanting to impress the King said, "Oh yes I have one daughter who is very beautiful and she can spin straw into gold."

"How interesting," said the King. "I am very short of gold at the moment. Send her to the palace immediately."

The miller ran home in a terrible state and told his daughter that she was to go to the palace and spin gold for the King. The poor girl was horrified.

"But father," cried the miller's daughter, "you know I cannot spin gold, how could you say such a thing?"

But the miller, thinking that he might lose his head if his daughter did not go, dragged her off to the castle.

When they reached the castle, the miller was sent home to his mill and his daughter was taken up to a small room in a tower where there stood a spinning wheel, a stool and a large pile of straw. The miller's daughter was told that she must spin all the straw into gold before the morning or she would die. The door was locked and the unhappy girl was left alone.

The miller's daughter knew quite well that she could not possibly spin the straw into gold and was so overcome with fear that she began to weep bitterly. Later that night the door of that little room softly opened and in came the strangest man. He was very small and had a long grey beard and he wore odd green clothes.

"Why are you weeping?" asked the little man.

"I have to spin all this straw into gold," sobbed the girl, "and as I cannot do this I shall die tomorrow."

"Perhaps I can help you," said the little man. "What will you give me if I spin the straw into gold for you?"

The miller's daughter offered him her necklace, which was made of fine blue beads. The little man seemed pleased with the necklace. He sat down at the spinning wheel and began to spin the straw into gold. By sunrise there was a large pile of gold and the little man left as quietly as he had come.

The King was delighted when he saw the gold and the next night the miller's daughter was taken to another room filled with an even larger pile of straw and was told to spin this into gold. The girl was left looking at the pile of straw wondering what she should do. But once more the odd little man came into the room and said he would

50

spin the straw into gold if the girl would give him something. The girl offered him her pearl ring and the little man sat down and spun all the straw into gold by the morning.

When the King saw the gold his longing for gold became greater. The next evening the miller's daughter was taken to another room in which there was an even larger amount of straw and the King told her that it was all to be spun into gold by the morning. The miller's daughter sat miserably on the stool and looked hopelessly at the straw. But once again the little man entered the room and said he would spin the straw into gold if the miller's daughter would reward him.

"But I have nothing left," said the miller's daughter.

"Well," said the little man, "if I turn this straw into gold for you, will you promise me your firstborn child after you have married the King?" The miller's daughter, although rather astonished at this request, was so desperate she agreed and the little man spun all the straw into gold.

The King was so impressed by the girl's magical abilities and finding her beautiful and agreeable asked her to be his wife.

Twelve months after the marriage the Queen gave birth to a strong baby boy. The King and Queen were delighted and the King found that he loved his wife and child more than all the gold that had been spun from the straw.

One day the Queen was sitting in her bed-chamber with the baby when, to her horror, the strange little man appeared in the room and claimed the baby. The Queen

fell to her knees and begged the little man not to take the child. She was so distraught that the little man took pity on her and said that if she could guess his name within three days she could keep the baby.

The Queen lay awake all that night thinking of every name she had ever heard. She even sent a messenger all over the kingdom to inquire what other names there were. When the little man appeared the next day the Queen began reciting all the names, beginning with Caspar, Melchior and Balthazar. But whatever name she mentioned the little man shook his head. The second day the messenger was sent off again to make more inquiries in the villages and to ask if there were any unusual names. When the little man came the Queen said, "is your name Cowribs, or Spiderlegs or even Spindle-shanks?" But everytime he answered, "no, that's not my name."

On the third day the messenger came to the Queen and said, "I haven't found any more names but high on the mountain, near where the eagle perches, I saw a small wooden house with a fire burning in front of it. And a ridiculous little man was dancing around the fire singing:

"Today I brew, today I bake,
Tomorrow the Queen's fair child I'll take,
My body's small, my legs are thin,
My name is Rumpelstiltskin."

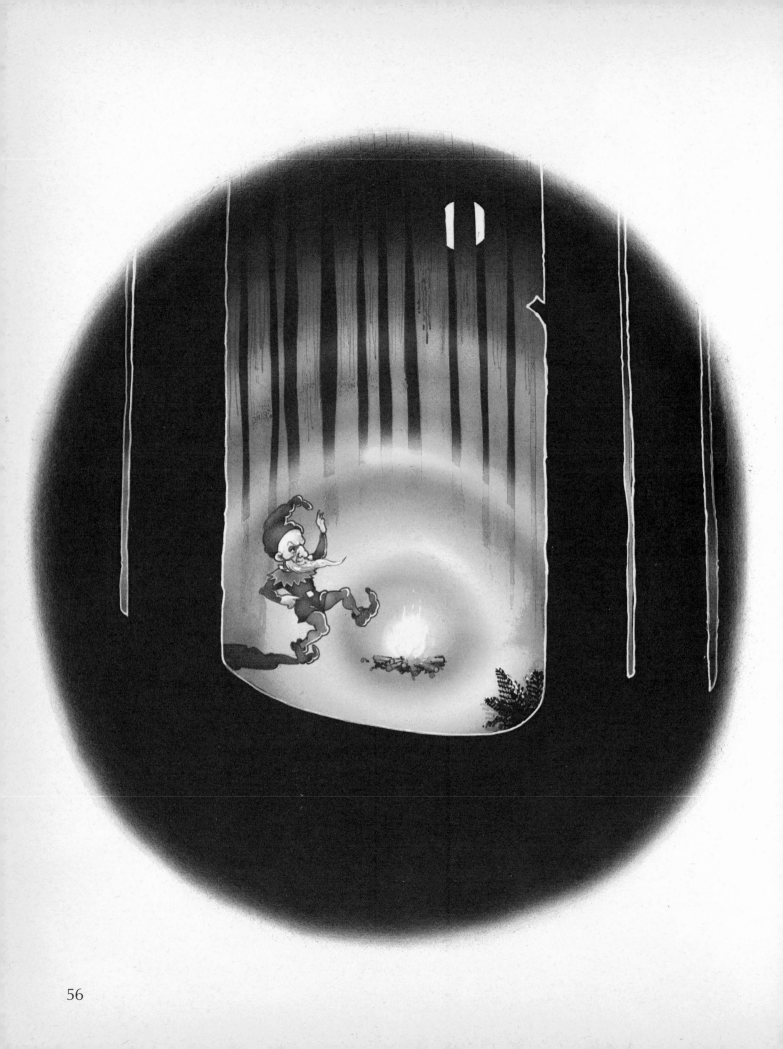

The Queen was delighted when she heard the name. Soon afterwards the little man came in.

"Is your name Tom?" said the Queen.

"No."

"Is your name Dick?"

"No."

"Is it perhaps, Rumpelstiltskin?"

The little man shrieked with rage and twirled round and round the room until he disappeared and was never seen again.

Goldilocks and the Three Bears

Once upon a time there was a little girl who lived in a pretty house on the edge of a large wood. She had long golden hair and was called Goldilocks. One morning Goldilocks woke up and found that the sun was streaming through her bedroom window.

"What a lovely morning," thought Goldilocks. "I shall go for a long walk through the wood." So she jumped out of bed, put on her favorite pink dress and while her mother was in the kitchen, slipped out through the front door. She ran down the garden path, through the garden gate, over the bridge which went across the stream and into the wood.

Right in the middle of this wood stood the sweetest cottage you can imagine. It was small and white and had roses climbing up the walls. The front door was yellow, and there were yellow shutters each side of the windows. The cottage belonged to three bears; Daddy Bear, who was very large; Mummy Bear, who was medium-sized; and Baby Bear, who was very small.

On this particular morning, Mummy Bear had made porridge for their breakfast. A large bowl for Daddy Bear, a medium bowl for herself, and a very small bowl

for Baby Bear. But it was too hot for the Bear family to eat, so they decided to go for a walk while the porridge cooled.

Goldilocks, meanwhile, had walked a long way through the wood and was very tired and hungry. When she came to the clearing where the Bear's cottage was, she thought perhaps the people who lived there might give her something to eat. So she went to the front door and knocked. Goldilocks banged three times, but there was no answer, so she peeped in through the windows. The table was set for breakfast, with three delicious bowls of porridge just waiting for someone to eat them.

So this naughty little girl climbed in through the window and went straight to the table. First she picked up Daddy Bear's spoon and tried his porridge, but...

"Oh, it's too hot, it's burnt my mouth," cried Goldilocks.

Then she tried Mummy Bear's porridge, but...

"Oh, it's too cold," she said this time.

Then she started eating Baby Bear's porridge and it tasted so nice that Goldilocks ate every bit.

When she had finished eating she felt rather tired and looked round for a chair to sit in.

First, she sat on Daddy Bear's chair, but it was much too hard and uncomfortable. Then she sat on Mummy Bear's chair, but that was much too soft, and Goldilocks sank right into it. So she sat on Baby Bear's chair, but alas Goldilocks was much bigger than Baby Bear and she broke his chair.

Still feeling tired, Goldilocks went upstairs into the

Bears' bedroom. She lay on each of the beds in turn. Daddy Bear's bed was too high. Mummy Bear's bed was too low, but Baby Bear's bed was so warm and cosy that Goldilocks curled up on it and was soon fast asleep.

Not long afterwards the Bears came home. They were very hungry. Daddy Bear looked at his bowl of porridge, saw the spoon in it and said in his gruff voice, "Someone has been eating my porridge." Mummy Bear looked at her porridge and said in her medium voice, "Someone has been eating my porridge." Baby Bear looked at his porridge and said in his little voice, "Someone has been eating my porridge, and they've eaten it all up."

Daddy Bear looked round the room, and saw the cushions crumpled on his chair and said, "Someone has been sitting in my chair." Mummy Bear looked at her chair and said, "Someone has been sitting in my chair." Baby Bear looked at his chair and cried, "Someone has been sitting in my chair and they've broken it," and he burst into tears.

Daddy Bear led the way upstairs, looked at his bed and saw that the bedclothes had been pulled back.

"Someone has been sleeping in my bed," he said. Mummy Bear looked at her bed. "Someone has been sleeping in my bed," said she.

Baby Bear looked at his bed and became so excited that he shouted, "Someone has been sleeping in my bed, and she's still there!"

He made so much noise that he woke Goldilocks up. She opened her eyes sleepily and to her horror found

that she was surrounded by three bears. Without waiting to thank them for the porridge, or to say sorry for breaking Baby Bear's chair, she sprang from the bed and jumped out of the window. Back through the wood she ran, over the bridge that went over the stream, through the garden gate, up the garden path and into her own house. And she never wandered into the wood by herself ever again.

Mummy Bear made some more porridge, Daddy Bear sat down with his hammer and nails and mended Baby Bear's chair, and Baby Bear made the beds. He felt a little sad that the pretty girl had not stopped to play with him and hoped that he might see her again one day.

Rapunzel

Once upon a time there lived a husband and wife who had no children. They were very sad about this and the wife would spend many hours gazing out of the window at the garden next door in which there were rows of delicious looking vegetables. One day the wife said to the husband, "Unless I can taste some of those vegetables I shall surely die."

She wept so sorely that her husband agreed to climb over the garden wall and fetch some for her. He was very frightened, for the garden belonged to an unpleasant old woman, who was supposed to be a witch. However, late that night he climbed over the wall, quickly picked some vegetables, and hastily climbed back again. His wife ate the vegetables and said that she must have some more; she could not live without them. So the poor man went once more into the witch's garden. But just as he was about to gather the vegetables, to his horror he found the witch standing beside him.

"What are you doing in my garden? Are you trying to steal my vegetables?" she hissed.

The terrified man explained about his wife.

"Well," said the old witch, "you may have the vege-

tables, but in return you must promise to give me your first born child."

Trembling, the man gave his promise and hastened back to his wife. He gave her the vegetables and told her of his awful promise.

Some months later the wife gave birth to a beautiful baby girl and that very day the old witch came to the house to claim the child. In spite of the husband's pleas the witch took her away.

The witch named the child Rapunzel and kept her until she was twelve years old. Then, wishing to hide her beauty from others, she shut her in a tall tower which had only one window and no door. Rapunzel had very long golden hair, so long that it reached to the bottom of the tower. Every evening Rapunzel braided her hair. When the witch came to the bottom of the tower and called "Rapunzel, Rapunzel let down your hair," she would drop the plait out of the window for the witch to climb up.

Shut in the tower Rapunzel was often lonely and would spend hours singing at the window. One evening a prince was riding through the forest and heard her lovely voice. He stopped his horse amongst some trees and looked to see who the maiden was who sang so sweetly. To his amazement he saw an old woman and heard her call out from the bottom of the tower, "Rapunzel, Rapunzel let down your hair." Then a long plait of golden hair fell from the window and the old woman climbed up it. The prince returned home but could not forget what he had seen. He was determined to meet the owner of the lovely voice. The next evening

he went to the tower and called out softly, "Rapunzel, Rapunzel let down your hair."

The plait came tumbling down and the prince climbed up it. He came face to face with the most beautiful girl he had ever seen. At first Rapunzel was very frightened, but after they had talked for a while she came to like the prince. The prince visited Rapunzel for many months after that and they fell in love. He brought Rapunzel skeins of silk so that she could make herself a silken ladder to escape from the tower.

But alas one evening Rapunzel said to the old witch, "Why is it that you are so much heavier than my prince?"

The witch was furious. "You shameful girl," she cried. "I thought I had hidden you from the whole world," and cut off Rapunzel's long golden hair and sent her off into the wilderness. When the prince arrived that evening and called to Rapunzel, the plait came down as usual but, at the window, instead of his beautiful Rapunzel, there was the hideous old witch.

"Your Rapunzel is dead," she laughed, "and you will see her no more."

The prince, in his misery, jumped from the tower, and was blinded as he fell into some thorn bushes. He wandered for many years but Rapunzel at last discovered him. She ran forward and clasped him in her arms and as her tears of joy fell on to his face his eyes were healed. They returned to the prince's kingdom, and were married and lived happily ever after.

Beauty and the Beast

Once upon a time there lived a very rich merchant who had three daughters. The youngest was called Beauty.

One day the merchant heard that all his ships had been lost at sea. He was now penniless, so he sold his fine house and carriages to pay his debts and with his daughters moved into a small cottage in the country.

His two elder daughters did not enjoy being poor. But Beauty in her ragged clothes quite happily learnt to cook, wash and clean, which was just as well for her elder sisters were so lazy.

One day the merchant received news that he might have the chance of saving some of his fortune.

"I must go to the port where my ship lies at anchor. What presents shall I bring you?" he asked his daughters.

"We want some new dresses, shoes and jewellery," cried the elder daughters. But all Beauty asked for was a single red rose.

The merchant rode away and when he had gone Beauty's two sisters laughed at her.

"Fancy asking for a single rose when you could have something rich and fine," they jeered.

When the merchant arrived at the port he found the

ship was not his; he was as poor as ever. So he set off home with a heavy heart. There was no hope of him retrieving the money and he had no gifts for his daughters. He rode on during the day, but towards evening dark clouds gathered. The wind began to howl among the trees and thick snow started to fall. Soon the merchant was completely lost in a large, dark forest. He became very cold and weak from hunger. He had given up hope of surviving, when he saw a light streaming from a window in a vast castle hidden among the trees.

The merchant urged his tired horse towards the light. He entered the courtyard of the castle and led his horse to a stable where he found blankets and food. When he had settled his horse for the night the merchant went into the castle. There was no-one to greet him, but the merchant was so exhausted that he stumbled down one of the long corridors, found a richly furnished bedroom, fell into bed and went straight to sleep.

In the morning the merchant set out through the castle to find the prince to thank him for his hospitality. He met no one so he went into the gardens.

They were as empty as the castle and the merchant was about to give up his search when he saw a rose bush with a beautiful red rose on it.

"This is just what Beauty wanted," thought the merchant, and he plucked the rose from the bush. Then he heard a terrible roar behind him and turned to find the most hideous creature.

"Oh, miserable, wretched man," growled the Beast. "You sleep in my castle, stable your horse in comfort, and

repay me by stealing the thing I love best in the world. You will pay with your life."

The merchant, his voice trembling, explained that he had picked the rose for his daughter Beauty. He begged the Beast to let him return home.

"On one condition," replied the Beast, "that you return in three months with your daughter."

The old man was so terrified that he agreed. When he reached home his daughters ran to greet him but the merchant turned away and wept. His two elder daughters kept asking for their presents so he had to tell them the dreadful story. Beauty tried to comfort him.

"I will go to the Beast and offer myself instead," he said. "I am old. My life no longer matters."

But Beauty would not hear of such a thing. After three months she and her father set off for the Beast's castle. Her two sisters tried to look sad, but they were really pleased to see her go as they were so jealous of her.

By nightfall Beauty and her father reached the castle. The merchant put the horses in the stable and took his daughter into the castle. In the large banqueting hall a splendid feast was laid. They sat down at the table and when supper was over the Beast appeared suddenly before them. Beauty shuddered at his terrifying appearance, but the Beast spoke gently to her and told her to think of herself as mistress of the castle. He said that she must bid farewell to her father in the morning. The merchant and Beauty spent the night talking and in the morning he rode away with many tears and sighs.

Beauty wandered sadly through the castle, but after

a while she found many treasures, fine pictures and books that interested her. That evening she found supper laid in the banqueting hall. As she sat down to eat, the Beast appeared and asked if he could sit with her while she ate. He spoke very gently and Beauty agreed.

"Do you find me very ugly?" the Beast asked.

"I do," said Beauty, "but I do not find you as frightening as I thought I would."

Every evening the Beast joined Beauty at supper. She became very fond of him and looked forward to his visits. One night the Beast asked Beauty to marry him, but she shrank away in horror and cried, "No, never."

The Beast gave Beauty a magic mirror so that she could see her family. One day she saw in it her father ill in bed.

"Please let me go to him," she begged.

"Very well," said the Beast, "but you must return in eight days or I shall die."

"I promise, I promise," cried Beauty.

The Beast gave her a magic ring and told her to shut her eyes and wish she were home. When Beauty opened her eyes she found herself in the cottage. How pleased she was to be home; but her sisters were envious of her fine clothes and her fine castle home. Beauty nursed her father back to health and at the end of eight days she prepared to return to the castle. But her two sisters were so jealous of their father's love for Beauty that they plotted to keep her at home.

"The Beast will be so angry with Beauty that he will destroy her," they said to each other.

"Do not go back to the Beast," they begged Beauty, "our father will surely die if you return and we will be heartbroken."

So Beauty said she would stay a few more days. But one night she dreamt vividly that the Beast was dying. In the morning she touched the magic ring, and wished herself back in the castle. She found the Beast in the gardens stretched out beneath a tree as if he was dead. Beauty ran to him and cried, "Don't die Beast, for I now know I love you as you are," and she bent to kiss him.

No sooner had she uttered these words than the Beast turned into a handsome young prince.

"You have broken the spell with these words of love," said the prince joyfully. "A wicked witch cast this spell on me years ago and it could only be broken by a girl who loved me as I am."

The merchant and Beauty's two sisters were summoned to the castle. Amidst great happiness and rejoicing Beauty and her prince were married. They lived happily ever after.

The Princess and the Pea

Many years ago there lived a very handsome prince. He dwelt with his father and mother, the King and Queen, in a very splendid castle. When the prince came of age it was decided that he should marry. But the prince was a very fussy young man and said that he would marry only a true princess. So the King and Queen sent off invitations to every neighbouring kingdom asking all the young maidens to come to a ball.

Duly they all arrived dressed in their best dresses. Thin girls, fat girls, fair ones, dark ones, pretty ones and ugly ones, but although the prince danced with every one not a single real princess could he find. The disappointed maidens all trooped home and the prince, very heartsore and footsore, decided that he must go to find his own princess.

The prince set out on horseback. He spent many months in many strange and distant countries seeking his princess but though he met many beautiful girls he still could not find a true princess. At last he returned home and told his mother and father he had given up all hope of ever finding one.

One night, some weeks later, the King, Queen and

prince were seated at dinner when they heard someone knocking at the front door. It was a very stormy night—the wind was howling round the turrets of the castle and the rain was beating against the windows.

"Some poor traveler must be lost in the darkness of the storm," said the King. "I will go and see if I can help them."

The King got up from the table and went to the front door. When he opened it there before him stood a beautiful young maiden. She was extremely wet, water dripped from her hair, from her dress and even her dainty little shoes were full of water.

"Oh, please help me," she cried, "I'm wet and cold and I've lost my way. And I'm a real princess," she added, managing to look dignified in spite of all the drips.

The King hastily told her to come in out of the wet and rushed off to find the Queen.

"Come quickly," he gasped, "it's a young girl and she says she is a real princess."

"We'll see about that," said the Queen, and went to welcome their guest.

"Come my dear," said she, "you must have a hot, bath, some food and then you must go to bed. You must be tired out."

She summoned servants to look after the girl. And when she had gone the Queen rushed off to the spare bedroom. She ordered the servants to lay twenty mattresses on the bed and twenty more feather mattresses on top of them. Then the Queen put a pea beneath them all. When the princess had bathed and eaten her supper the

Queen led her to the bedroom, tucked her into bed and wished her goodnight.

"Now we will see whether she is a true princess or not," said the Queen to herself and went back to her dinner.

The next morning the princess appeared at breakfast looking very tired and wobegone.

"Whatever is the matter," said the Queen, "didn't you sleep well my dear?"

"No, indeed I didn't," said the princess, "there was something very hard in my bed, I tossed and turned all night and I am bruised black and blue." And the poor girl started to cry.

"You are truly a real princess," said the Queen. "Only a real princess would have such delicate feelings that her sleep would be ruined by a pea." The prince was overjoyed that he had at last found his real princess and, as she was beautiful and good, fell in love with her and they married and lived happily all their lives. The pea was placed in a museum and lies there still for people to come and wonder at.

Ali Baba and the Forty Thieves

A long time ago in a land called Persia, there lived two brothers, Ali Baba andCassim. Ali Baba was a poor woodcutter, but his brother had married a wealthy wife so they saw very little of each other.

One morning Ali Baba set off into the forest on his daily task of gathering firewood to sell in the market. He had just finished loading the wood on to his small donkey when he heard the sound of horses galloping towards him. Thinking that they might be robbers Ali Baba decided to hide. He tethered the donkey behind a bush and quickly climbed up a tree.

He watched closely as they passed beneath him. The leader was a richly dressed man, with a cruel dark face, who carried a large, sharp scimitar at his side. The other thirty-nine men looked equally dangerous, so Ali Baba stayed very quietly in his tree. The leader stopped his horse before a large slab of rock and to Ali Baba's amazement uttered the words "Open Sesame." The rock at once slid open revealing a cave wide enough to allow the horsemen to enter four abreast. When they were all inside, the rock returned to its former position. Ali Baba thought it wise to stay where he was and was glad he had

done so, for before long the rock moved again and out came the forty thieves. When they had disappeared into the forest, Ali Baba slid down the tree and nervously approached the rock. "Open Sesame", said he in a trembling voice and the rock obligingly slid open.

Ali Baba entered the cave and found himself surrounded by the most glittering array of treasure: enough riches to make a dozen sultans happy. There were chests of gold and silver pieces, boxes of glittering jewels, rich silks, furs and brocades.

Ali Baba wasted no time in filling his pockets with gold, silver and jewels. He then stood before the rock door and said, "Open Sesame." The rock opened and Ali Baba went out into the clearing. He emptied the firewood from the panniers on his donkey and going back into to the cave filled them with treasure. He then mounted the donkey and returned home as quickly as possible.

His wife was rather anxious about him as he was usually home in time for supper. But she soon forgot her worries when Ali Baba showed her the baskets full of riches and told her about the robber's cave.

"Now help me to bury it beneath the floorboards," said Ali Baba to his wife. But she begged him to let her measure it. "I will borrow a measuring cup from Cassim's wife. It seems a shame not to know just how much gold we have."

Ali Baba agreed, but told his wife not to tell anyone of their good fortune. "If Cassim finds out," he said, "he will want to go to the cave and then the robbers will know and come after us."

Cassim's wife was very curious when the wood-cutter's wife came rushing into her house asking for a measuring cup. "I can't tell you anything," said Ali Baba's wife, "just give me the cup." So Cassim's wife went into the kitchen to fetch the cup, but before she gave it to Ali Baba's wife, she rubbed grease on to the bottom of it. When Ali Baba's wife returned it the next morning, she did not notice that there was a gold coin stuck to the cup. When Cassim saw this he ran straight to his brother's house and found Ali Baba burying the last of the gold. He forced him to tell the whole story and when he heard of all the treasure his eyes gleamed greedily. In spite of his brother's pleas to be cautious, Cassim rode straightaway to the cave. He shouted, "Open Sesame," the rock moved to one side and Cassim entered. The treasure was beyond his wildest dreams and he spent far too much time in selecting a vast collection of gold, silver and jewels. But alas, when he at last came to his senses and decided it would be prudent to leave, he could not remember the magic password. He was trapped in the cave and before long the robbers returned. Cassim tried to hide at the back of the cave, but they soon discovered him and the robber-chief, unmoved by his pleas for mercy, killed him.

Meanwhile Ali Baba, worried by the length of time his brother had been away, went to the cave. When he entered the cave he found his brother dead upon the floor. With a heavy heart he took the body to Cassim's wife and made her swear that she would never reveal how Cassim had died.

But the robbers, finding that the body had been

removed from their hiding place, knew that yet another had discovered their secret. The robber-chief went into the town and pretending to be an oil-merchant, found that Ali Baba, once a poor woodcutter, was now a man of considerable fortune. The chief guessed that this was the man who knew the password and was determined to have his revenge.

He went to Ali Baba's house still in his disguise of an oil-merchant. Ali Baba was delighted to have so distinguished a guest and invited him to stay the night. During the afternoon, when no-one else was in the house, the other thirty-nine robbers crept into the house and hid themselves in some empty oil jars in the kitchen. In the evening Morgiana, Ali Baba's slave-girl, went to the oil jars to fetch oil for use in preparing the feast to be held in honour of the oil-merchant. To her horror, when she lifted the lid a voice asked, "Is it time yet?" Recovering her senses the girl replied, "Not yet." From each jar she received the same question and to each she gave the same answer. She now realized that these were robbers and they meant to kill her master. She crept away and returned with kettles of boiling oil, which she poured into the jars, killing all the robbers.

Later that evening, while she was waiting on Ali Baba and his guest, she caught the glimpse of a dagger beneath the oil merchant's cloak. Morgiana knew that this must be the robber-chief. She went to her master and asked if she could dance for his guest after dinner. Ali Baba agreed, knowing how much her dancing pleased his son. After dinner Morgiana changed into her most

glittering costume and holding a jewelled dagger began her dance. She whirled around the room and as she passed in front of the robber-chief she leapt towards him and plunged the dagger into his heart.

Ali Baba was horrified, and leapt to his feet. "Why have you done this?" he cried.

Morgiana lifted the robber-chief's cloak and showed her master the dagger. She then told Ali Baba the whole story and Ali Baba was overcome with gratitude.

"How can I reward such a loyal and brave slave?" he asked.

Before Morgiana could reply, his son said, "Free her, father, so that we can be married."

Ali Baba consented and as a wedding present told the happy pair the secret password for the cave, so that all the treasure would be theirs.